John Savage

Eva

A Goblin Romance in Five Parts

John Savage

Eva
A Goblin Romance in Five Parts

ISBN/EAN: 9783337048297

Printed in Europe, USA, Canada, Australia, Japan

Cover: Foto ©Andreas Hilbeck / pixelio.de

More available books at **www.hansebooks.com**

EVA:

A GOBLIN ROMANCE,

IN FIVE PARTS.

BY

JOHN SAVAGE,

AUTHOR OF "SYBIL, A TRAGEDY," "FAITH AND FANCY,"
ETC., ETC.

NEW YORK:

JAMES B. KIRKER,

(LATE EDWARD DUNIGAN & BROTHER,)

599 BROADWAY, (UP STAIRS.)

1865.

TO

ROBERT SHELTON MACKENZIE, D. C. L.

My Dear Doctor:—

I feel a pardonable pride in offering you this little book. Were its merits but equal to the gratification experienced in dedicating it to you, its reputation would be a foregone conclusion, and only make me more happy that it was in some degree worthy of your acceptance. I pray you, however, to take it, such as it is, as a small token of my appreciation of your indefatigable labors in the cultivation and dissemination of a healthy and hearty Polite Literature, of your high sense of professional independence, and of your generosity to professional juniors—a generosity the more gladly recorded here because I have been a partaker of its fruits.

Among contemporary writers, I am not aware of any more ready to welcome and endorse what your judgment recognizes as deserving: or who, being forced into an opposite course, justifies his disapproval out of resources more complete, or by standards more compatible with common sense and the dignity of letters. These characteristics, so widely valued and respected, fortify the desire of personal regard to inscribe this romance with your name.

A word as to the work itself. While illustrating the plot— if I may call it such—by the resources Fancy and Imagination conjure up as lying within the supernatural and fairy realms, and by the reflection of the scenery, occasion, and moods of the actors upon each other, I have attempted—like an old-fashioned story-teller—more than once to point a moral; and in the con-

1*

cluding part, to lead the mind to dwell on the still higher, more enduring, and more consoling teaching of Christianity, that, amid the vicissitudes which rack man—not the least crushing of which is a transition from the egotistic rapture of a passionate young love to the humiliating consciousness of moody despair—his only comfort and lasting reward is to be found in the self-sacrifice, the resignation—in a word—the humble, but heroic virtues symbolized by The Cross.

Accept, my dear Doctor, this dedication, with the affectionate esteem of

Your Friend,

John Savage.

Fordham, *September* 25, 1865.

EVA.

PART FIRST.

I.

Tue evening Sun was setting fair
   Beneath a sky of blue,
And Nature's charms on earth, in air,
   Were fading into dew:

II.

The sun's broad beams athwart did lie
   The crimson-mantled West,
As a golden Cross of Chivalry
   Charged on a purple vest:

III.

The evening star, with tender freight
　Of charitable mirth,
Did seem to cheer and gratulate
　The day-tired sons of earth.

IV.

A gentle breath the shrubs among—
　A gentle sigh of air.
As though a gentle maiden's song
　Was lilting here and there;

V.

The busy bushes keeping time,
　The tendrils join each note,
And all is soft as silv'ry rhyme
　From out a silv'ry throat:

VI.

The grass assumes a whimpering thrill
　As through it wings the wind,
So gently though, it scarcely speeds
To coax a chorus from yon weeds,
　Ere all is still behind:

VII.

The dry stems wheeze a tiny pipe
　　To show they wakeful lie,
As urchins mumble unknown type
　　When pedagogue struts by:

VIII.

The wild rose blushes on the eve
　　Of going to its rest,
And bends its crimson cheek to grieve
　　On mother Earth's calm breast.

IX.

The dew steals o'er primroses pale
　　Which deck yon shady place;
And clustering in a shy delight,
Help to shake the tears of night
　　From off each others' face:

X.

And hawthorn blossoms titter low,
　　For fear their joyannce reach
The matron-like and crabbed boughs,
While am'rous Air essays its vows
　　And steals a kiss from each:

XI.

The mountain Ash, gay lithe and young,
   With knowledge of its grace,
Unheedful hears the gallant's song,
Nor cares be won by secret tongue,
   It bends to bolder face.

XII.

The evening calm as the smile of Him,
   Who said, " Thy Will be done,"
And the pious air seemed hushed in prayer
   Like a seraphic nun.

XIII.

The scene was wild, yet Fancy made
   Its features full of balm
As though it joined the lengthening shade
   To make the day's death calm.

XIV.

In truth it was a placid scene
   Where awe did wonder woo:
Yea, such as men full seldom ken
   The coming twilight through.

XV.

It is a brocken valley wild,
  The Dodder streaming down
Its centre, and the mountain heath
Envelops with a purple wreath
  Kippure's age-mottled crown.

XVI.

O valley! consecrate to song,
  In poet-warrior's soul,
Where memories of Ossian throng—
  Delightful Glau-nis-mole![1]

XVII.

O valley! famed in Ancient days
  Not more by Ossian's voice,
Than thrushes', whose bewildering maze
Of melody made all thy braes
  And hundred dells rejoice.

XVIII.

Romantic, rugged, sombre, grand,
  The hills jut out and fall
Into the devious vale, as though
To stay the Dodder's reckless flow:
  Which, foams, and frets, through all.

XIX.

They drive the stream from shore to shore;
　　It shakes with rage, then sweeps
Around the base, with lengthening pace,
With sullen surge, breaks through the gorge,
　　And frothing, onward leaps.

XX.

By Alyagower, clear as glass
　　The pools glide smoothly free,
Till further down, a group of rocks,
Like bathing dwarfs, jumps up and mocks
　　Their placid ecstasy.

XXI.

Then like branch-broken rays from sun—
　　Or sparks from the blacksmith's blow—
Or, shattered gems, they flash and run
　　To frothen the angry flow.

XXII.

And now they chant a boisterous song,
　　United, now they hymn,
And anon they murmuring lilt along
　　In the shade of yon brocken, dim.

XXIII.

The brave ship many leagues must tack
  As air and ocean wills:
So strove the river, making track
  Athrough this sea of hills.

XXIV.

An ivy-quilted scanty ruin
  Lies hugged i' the valley wild;
And tombs there tell, of all save hell
  To martyr, man, and child.

XXV.

In the shade of the lonely pile,
  Like life within a dream,
In the shade of the holy aisle
  A listening to the stream—

XXVI.

A listening to the Dodder's woes
  A-neath the ivy green,
A damsel and youth, the like in sooth
  I'm sure you ne'er have seen.

XXVII.

Ye sprites, it was a dreamy scene.
　And a witching wild one, too,
Such as we but seldom see,
　The elfin twilight through.

．

XXVIII.

The youthful maid an angel's face—
　And angel's form, I ween,
A mingling grace lit up her face
　Of blooming ripe sixteen.

XXIX.

Tresses like an autumn night
　Hang o'er her forehead's day,
Darkly rich—a pearly light
　Outlines each curling spray

XXX.

Eyes of such unearthly light,
　Though dark as ever wrought;
By Heaven! they twist me as a sprite,
　Though I but see in thought.

XXXI.

Much more they twisted yon poor soul,
   The brave youth by her side,
Whose pupils rise to the maid's dark eyes
And in the wild glance dies, and dies
   To live in hopeful pride.

XXXII.

He sighs, that wily nature should
   Play freaks to show her might,
And make in witching maidenhood
   The darkest eyes most bright.

XXXIII.

Her forehead, as white marble, pale,
   The veins an azure river,
Where tints of Ireland's skies prevail
   In softness, softening ever.

XXXIV.

Her cheeks, the dainty tenderness
   As when at morning's dawn,
The sun-beam is shed, through a rose-leaf, red,
   On a neighboring ceanavaun.[2]

XXXV.

Her lips! a healthy pure repast—
    A sylph's or mortal's, which?
The upper like the bright spring cast,
    The under autumn rich:

XXXVI.

And both control a fragrant breath
    Like breeze o'er summer flowers,
When jocund morn enliveneth
    Earth's re-awakened powers.

XXXVII.

Her voice was like a happy thought
    Whose speaking smile did sun you,
And ere you heard the opening word
    The movement had undone you.

XXXVIII.

A raiment white with girdle green
    Her dainty waist about,
For as her heart was pure within,
    Her garb was pure without.

XXXIX.

So take the fair for all in all :
  Such a pure though tempting smile,
Ne'er shone from maid
As on him who strayed
  Through that old monastic aisle.

XL.

Comely shaped the youth, and slender ;
  With four summers o'er her own :
    And ever since they gambolled
    On the hill-paths over-brambled,
In sunny childhood's days, the tender
  Passion, with their growth had grown.

XLI.

Never slept it : for their sleeping
  Ne'er was by its dreams forsaken—
    Sleep, our Nature's El Dorado,
    Only held it by a shadow—
While they gathered golden dream-tales
  To be told when they'd awaken.

2*

XLII.

Thus their nights were but as segments
  Of the circle of their days;
And their young hearts, sunny centres,
  Rich with Love's converging rays.

XLIII.

Young Kevin Dhu, so was he hight,
  For ay, was youth as good
As e'er bent bow on Saxon foe,
Or boasted the commingling flow
  Of Celto-Norman blood.

XLIV.

His voice is full and freshly clear
  As the breeze on Comm'ragh's crown;
His hand can harp to a maiden's ear
  Or strike a foeman down.

XLV.

The brown locks cluster on his brow,
  Like grapes on the brow of Pan,
And you see a man in the youth though now
  The youth is scarcely man.

XLVI.

Lonely looks the ancient pile ;
　　But love is lonely never,
When loving eyes exchange the while
　　The arrows from Love's quiver.

XLVII.

Solemn the weird and lonely scene,
　　Solemn the tombs arraigned—
It looks as Life had all buried been,
　　And they alone remained.

XLVIII.

In truth, it was a holy scene,
　　And a lonely wild one too,
Such as men full seldom ken
　　The dusky twilight through.

XLIX.

A harp, Love's vibrant symbol, rude
　　In shape, but sweet in tone,
Lay o'er a tomb, as though its mood
　　Was dirging the dead alone.

L.

She sate her down upon a tomb,
  A cross rose high before,
With mossy shapes from Time's gray womb,
  Emboss'd and stained o'er.

LI.

"What hopes!" he cried, "what love, what truth,
  These ancient crosses speak!
What chastening thoughts for strength and
    youth,
  What sinews for the weak!

LII.

"With Vandal Time, their Sculptures rude
  But sacred combat well;
Like trusty friends, they have outstood
  The wealth that from us fell.

LIII.

"'Twould seem the centuried bones beneath,
  With strength of faith had grown
To mark the true soul's hope in death,
  And rose in sculptured stone.

LIV.

" Ye granite graybeards of the past
　　Who watch our kindred o'er,
With us may e'er thy teachings last,
　　That we the Cross adore.

LV.

" These crosses, like great note-marks, stand
　　O'er all the Celtic sod,
Grown gray in agony of love
　　Referring us to God !"[3]

LVI.

And then, as dropping in the tide
　　Of thought his fervor sprung,
The youth in Celtic anguish sighed
　　Its mysty waves among.

LVII.

'Twas but a moment, though it seemed,
　　In retrospection, years,
And waking from the life he dreamed—
　　Ancestral blood and tears—

LVIII.

He leaned against the carven cross,
　That rood of holy stone,
In love's weird tremors both at loss,
　To claim each heart their own.

LIX.

He brushed his brow, he snatched his harp,
　A prelude wildly rang;
Then melting to a plaintive width
　Of soul, he to her sang:

(I.)

A love-lorn minstrel once there dwelt,
　In a valley fair to view,
Whose young rapt soul and senses knelt,
　A heavenly maid to woo.
His love was fierce as Saint Kevin's hate,[4]
　Pure as yon spring of Saint Ann,—
He loved with the fervor soul doth create,
　As a minstrel only can.

(II.)

He roamed like spirit called from earth,
　Chimed from its grave of rest,

Penance to eke for some worldlie mirth,
   Or for some act unblest :
For his love was fierce as Saint Kevin's hate,
   Killing as e'en the Saint's ban :
Oft voiceless, his was an ideal state
   Of loving, as minstrel can.

(III.)

He tracked her steps, o'er vale and hill,
   True as the shadow she made ;
He blessed the sod whereon she trod,
   And the breeze that round her played.
For never to him had the sense of sound
   So lovingly tender grown,
As when the air, caressing the fair,
   Partook of her dulcet tone.

(IV.)

The Holy Well at which she drank
   To him more holy grew
Each tree that gave her shade, each bank
   She rested on, he knew !
For he gazed on his love as Martyr would
   On the hope that raised his soul,
And his eyes to her rolled as the halo should
   Round the head of the Virgin roll.

(v.)

Oh, this maid was his sole divinity !
   A model for aye far above
Aught his brain, in its minstrel affinity
   To heaven, could weave for his love !
And he loved her as Kate loved Saint Kevin,
   And he traced her as dial the sun ;
For at morning, at noon, or at even,
   By either you'd find t'other one.

(vi.)

And though they had gambolled in youthhood,
   From childhood to each other clung,
Yet neither had strength in their truthhood,
   Nor perfectly freedom of tongue :
For love, when it grows up from childhood,
   Ne'er thinks to seek deeper the clue,
But looks on each face as the wildwood,
   Where unconscious their heart-flowers grew.

(vii.)

And though he had laughed forth his fancies,
   And though she reëchoed his tale,
Yet for *one* word each heart inward glances—
   That one word of blessing or bale.

LX.

" Ah, sad is the time !" spake Eva,
  " When hearts are unconsciously tost;
  'Twere better that one should have spoken
  Than voiceless that both should be lost.

LXI.

" Ah," sighed she, " I pain for the maiden !"
  " And I," quoth he, " wail for the youth !"
  " And did neither make them an Aiden,
  By shriving the other from ruth ?

LXII.

" And did neither think of presuming
  On friendship that from their birth grew ?"
" Ah, no !" said the young bard resuming
  His harp, and its love-burdened clue :

" Though the youth but in her saw his heaven,
  Still spake not, or heard not *the word ;*
  For," he faltered, " the youth's name was KEVIN,
  And—EVA, the maid he adored !"

3

LXIII.

With modest, not unconscious air,
  Dear Eva heard him close : —
And looked, but spoke not, worlds of prayer,
  That only true love knows.

LXIV.

She felt—she knew, she had *his* heart,
  And that it spake through her,
And waited her responsive part
  From *him*,—nor dared to stir,—

LXV.

Nor dared to stir, lest she displace
  The accents she well knew
Her heart must make ; but woke apace
  To her own maiden view.

LXVI.

"Ah, Kevin! in my maiden soul
  Is the heart that I bereft
Thee of—that I, unconscious, stole,—
  Yet, willing for the theft :

LXVII.

"Ay, willing for the theft! O youth,
　　O Kevin dear! 'tis frail
That Eva's tongue should tell; but truth
　　And love's a sad tell-tale."

LXVIII.

"Angel of Eva! let me hear
　　Those kindling thoughts again;
That Hope's clear light may shame the bier
　　Where chilling Doubt lies slain!"

LXIX.

"My Kevin dear, fain would I tell,—
　　My tongue but shames its place,
My lips but mock the inward spell
　　That needs would outward trace.

LXX.

"My heart is throbbing like a sea,
　　And could sea span the skies above,
I feel its vast immensity
　　Could not cradle half my love."

LXXI.

Entrancèd in her speech, he gazed
    As though a statue still—
Or like a breathless sculptor, dazed
    At his creative skill.

LXXII.

But suddenly he started,—bright,
    His thankful gestures spoke,
As vocal as a host of light,
    In cave dawn never woke.

LXXIII.

His harp fell on the tufted moss,
    His tongue seemed in his fingers,[5]
That motion all his words,—at loss
    While speech on his dumb mouth lingers.

LXXIV.

He wrapt her to his burning breast,
    That love should fear no cheating;
He prest her, that each pledging test
    Should feel each other beating.

LXXV.

Exchangèd troths of love were given,
　And Echo sealed each tone,
Before the Cross, and the holy heaven,
　In the ivied ruin lone.

3*

PART SECOND.

I.

As thus the pair entrancèd were,
 Each with the other's love;
Unseen, unheard, about them there
 A horrid pageant wove.

II.

Old name-lost tombs 'gan start to life—
 The dead 'gan hobbling out,
Martyrs and monks, and man and wife,
 To witness what they're about.

III.

As lumberingly moved the mounds
 That did the ground encumber,
The headstones cracked their lichen skins,
 And yawn'd, like sots in slumber.

IV.

Old battered memories on the walls,
   Took shape and left their places;
Crushed effigies in crumbling stalls,
   Resumed their forms and faces.

V.

And skeletons helped with rattling noise
   To empty each other's graves,
To witness the troth and hear the voice
   Of love that daintily raves.

VI.

The oldest trees did shake and quake
   Up to their farthest shoots,
     As each skeleton pulls
     Might and main for the skulls,
Meshed in the tangled roots.

VII.

You'd think it was a lashing hail
   Upon the branching eaves;
Or wild despoiling autumn gale
   A throttling all the leaves.

VIII.

And while the groups are gathering round
   From out their dim abodes,
The woes and state of some create
   Grim ghastly episodes.

IX.

A horrid shape from the path to hell
   Escaped to quench his thirst,
For his inside scorch'd as flames do dwell
   In house pent ere they burst.

X.

He came to drink of the mystic Well
   Blessed by the good Saint Ann,
Whose waters boast the purest spell
   From Tallaght to Lough Dan.[6]

XI.

And deftly to the holy pool
   This ghastly shape forsooth
Did speed, with shrinèd wave to cool
   His hellish scorching drouth.

XII.

He snatched the bowl from the holy stone,
  And dived it in the Well;
    But yet while there flew
    His parched frame through
  A bliss from the hoped-for spell,
    A hurrying sprite
    Dashed the cup from his sight,
And he felt o'er again pangs of hell.

XIII.

Oh could he but drink of the shriving wave,
  'Twould give him the freedom of soul
To think of a heav'n; his body 'twould save
From the torturing pangs of a hell-bound grave:
  He snatches again at the bowl.

XIV.

Is it Saint Ann? or a guarding band?
  Or hath he a soul conscience-barred?
Again the cup from his flaming hand
  Is dashed by some unseen guard—

XV.

And a voice, like the rending of great forest oaks,
　Begat on his ear, with a yell,
The sentence of Fate—"Hence slave to your
　　state
　And your purgatorial cell."

XVI.

He shrunk aback, as his head had been
　Clove with Saint Peter's key,
And he durst not look, for bell and book
　Had told him where he would be.

XVII.

And a group kept watching a tomb in the aisle,
And they grinned a wrathful, vengeful smile,
　　In wait for its inmate's skull;
　　　　For he was a lord,
　　　　Whose only word
　　　　Was of hate to the poor,
　　　　And death to the boor
　　　　Who made not his door
　　And halls with venison full;

XVIII.

And oft had this baron been known to brag,
 The number of vassals he clove with his mace;
And he took less delight racing after the stag,
 Than he did in staying the human race.

XIX.

And one yelled forth a merry stave,
 A hundred choruss'd the verse;
  And from under a cowl,
  A relentless jowl
 Mumbled a hopeful curse.

XX.

And one whose flesh was half decayed
 Poured forth a troublous groan,
Which shook the slime from his wormy side,
 And bared it to the bone.

XXI.

Some had on cerements gray, which flapped
 As loose sails on the spars of a ship;
And some, half-rotted on what they wrapped,
 Were as cobwebs caught on a chip.

XXII.

One looked at her tomb as at her glass,
    Ne'er doubting herself 'twould bear,
        But she yelled her joy
        At the fond foul lie
    Her husband had sculptured there.

XXIII.

And calling a troupe of like wild wives,
    She bade them see themselves—
All scampered away as they did in their lives—
    A pack of mad vain elves.

XXIV.

And they laughed, did this brood of wanton
    wives,
    At their sculptured acts, and cried—
"Ho! ho! for those who have led good lives,
    They'll have no surprise when they've died."

XXV.

And as the "Yes" from Eva's mouth
    Proclaimed young Kevin's bride,
All swirled as though the grapes of the South
    Were gurgling their skulls inside.

4

XXVI.

And a jolly mob around the pair
    Prankt madly in a reel,
And chattered, and bowed, and flattered aloud,
    The lovers with devilish zeal.

XXVII.

But lovers' eyes, though ope are blind,
    And lovers' ears are deaf;
'Tis but in loving lovers find
    Love's grief or love's relief.

XXVIII.

Young Kevin clasped the maid again,
    The embrace was soft and sweet;
The bubbling love of the wooers twain,
    At parting was as they'd meet.

XXIX.

And as love's tender stupor sheds
    Its filmy mask, they thought
The air was dotted with strange heads,
    And with strange noises fraught.

XXX.

Their skinny digits clasping fast,
    The mouldy dancers spin
Swiftly past—their skulls are cast
    Into one circling grin.

XXXI.

The fluttering Eva nestled close
    Unto her Kevin's breast,—
They soothed the sudden fears that rose,
    By being both caressed.

XXXII.

" The noise"—it was the weary breeze,
    Or Dodder's plaining tones:
" The faces"—moonshine through the trees
    Upon the quaint old stones.

XXXIII.

And wilder, swifter speed the wraiths,
    As on a whirlpool leaves,
Until they fade, and the speering maid
    Feels she herself deceives.

XXXIV.

The moon breaks from her camp of clouds,
  And roams the clear expanse;
The ghosts glide into their slimy shrouds,
  Tired with the trysting dance.

PART THIRD.

I.

The moon was taking her highest roll,
　And the light from her regnant head,
Enwrapped the stars, like a mighty scroll,
　With eternity's language spread.

II.

The crystal blue of the ambient sky,
　The crystal light of the moon,
The crystal note of the black-bird nigh,
　Makes echo a crystal tune.

III.

The stars like strings of a heavenly lyre,
　Swept by the hands of Night,
Fill with joy the cathedral choir;
　And echo is turned to light.

IV.

And down the moonlight flutes the air,
　　Each beam a choral column ;
And earth's calm but responsive prayer
　　Blends in the midnight solemn.

V.

And heavenly smiles and earthly thanks
　　In their descent and upward flight,
Pass in joyed and bowèd ranks
　　Through night's corridors of light.

VI.

The wakeful crags, Kippure's broad brow
　　Stand out in bright relief,
Attendant on the moon ; and throw
　　The glens in shadowed grief.

VII.

Scarce a stir was up in the air,
　　Scarce a stir on the earth,
Save lyrical rills from the elfin hills
　　Gamb'lling in wildsome mirth.

VIII.

They staved and raved adown the stones,
　　A stop-note every pebble,
To quiver the chant into tinkling tones
　　Of a dulcet treble.

IX.

At the time of fair Eva's vows
　　To Kevin's love-lit power,
The elfin queen her courtiers did rouse
　　To meet over Alyagower.

X.

Bustling, yet noiseless, came along
　　The elves from midnight sprees,
Lowly but sweet as ever was song
　　They lilted their gathering glees:
So genial the flow, so num'rous the throng,
　　It was as a perfumed breeze—
Or, like a forethought of Zephyr's song,
　　Balmy, without the breeze.

XI.

As diamond thoughts in quaint bard's brain,
　　This aeriel world 'gan float;
And linked, as the gems of a fountain rain
　　By the mist, with a dewy note.

XII.

A haze of sound enwrapped the elves
 As the mist o'er a wayward stream ;
They must have thought, the imps themselves,
 They were in an elfin dream.

XIII.

And hither they come, so various dight—
 So brilliant their guises were,
It was as a sudden May that night,
 And they the flow'rs o' the air.

XIV.

Spirit of Heath and Daisy-dew,
 And tiny Blue-bell first,
Bounding came, with the elfin crew,
 That followed in a burst.

XV.

Honey-suckle and Primrose-tip,
 Arm in arm, I wist—
And Evening-sigh and Tulip-lip,
 And the Fog-sprite, Dodder-mist :

XVI.

Jessamine-breath and Woodbine-brow,
  Blessing each other's way,
And Honey-tongue and Folks-glove, now,
  And many a valley fay:

XVII.

The scarlet Dragon's-head came up,
  And Morning-glory too,
Bearing a monstrous purple cup
  Gleaming with nectrous dew:

XVIII.

And Apple-bloom so lustrous white,
  Like little bride of old;
And Dandelion, like ancient king,
  With collar of yellow gold:

XIX.

And from the Dodder's coolest vale
  The Brook-elf, braw and stout,
In armor made of a silver scale
  Dropped from a river trout:

XX.

The imp of glens, wild Thatchet-thorn,
    Reckless, rollicking sprite,
Came puffing, like a November morn
    Hunted by autumn night:

XXI.

The Moon-elf with a bright'ning eye,
    And never a wink, came in;
He trimm'd the starry lamps on high,
    And shaded the ways of sin.

XXII.

And Poppy-stem with night-cap red,
    A drowsy pace did take;
But Moon-elf kicked and Thatchet pricked
    The imp to keep him awake.

XXIII.

And hosts of elfin chiefs appeared
    Of marvellous renown,
And fairy seannachies[s] with beards
    Of silver thistle-down.

XXIV.

Oh, myriads came, of goblin fame,
  From glen-embower'd ways,
Where cascades keep the hills from sleep,
  In witching Wicklow's praise;
From Dodder's nooks, and brawling brooks,
  And Liffey's fairy braes.

XXV.

They came t. a tower, 'tween heav'n and earth,
  Built in the dewy air;
The dreamliest space that fanciful mirth
  Could deem for a court so rare.

XXVI.

They carried a cloud away up to the moon
  And trailed it across the light,
So the beam from below, and the beam from aboon,
  Made a floor and a ceiling bright.

XXVII.

And they sprent the floor with gathered dews
  Which shone like a pavement of gems,
    And arch'd columns made
    Of the clear cascade,
  Caught ere it broke in diadems.

XXVIII.

From quarried mines of perfume, the walls—
  The casement of spider's web, quaint,
    And the toiling stars
    Snatch a peep through the bars,
  And pale at their own restraint.

XXIX.

And o'er the throne of Cleena the queen,
  In the nave of this fairy pile,
    A tulip leaf rained
    Its hues, like the stained
  Glass saints in cathedral aisle.

XXX.

Thus met, the queen with an airy tongue,
  Like a sweet voice heard in a dream,
Half cadenced her will, half liltingly sung—
  Yet singing it only did seem.

XXXI.

  Oh, her's was the sweetest,
  Richest, completest,
  Most musical, magic, and dearest,
  Mystic and lowly,
  Swelling but slowly,
The warmest of voices, and clearest!

XXXII.

" Sisters and brothers—subjects all,
 From Tallaght to Kippure,
From the dusky valleys,
Where the sunset rallies,
All our gallant armies to my evening call—
From the heathy hill-side,
From the dreamy rill-side,
From the spray entrancing,
In the star-light glancing,
O'er the rocky barriers in the Dodder's way,—
Ye, my loved and loving,
Ye, the spry and roving,
Ye, that know a living dead to things of clay,
Ye, from Tallaght's meadows.
 To the bleak Kippure,
Ye, I want—my shadows!
 A maiden to secure.

XXXIII.

" Cluricauns from haunted Brake,
 Fays of Alyagower,
I've a maid from earth to take
 Worthy fairy power.

XXXIV.

" Wild elves from the witch'd Cornaun,
　　Whose broad brow the thunder mocks,
And all ye that wraithe Glancree,
　　Or guard the lonely haunted Loughs,—⁹

XXXV.

" Where the eagle mountain stands
　　O'er the dismal wave below;
Like man's suicidal thought
　　Brooding flight from earthly wo:

XXXVI.

" There is a maid of mildest mien,
　　But radiant in its mildness!
Loving and loved in the bounds atween,
　　Where we hold our wildness."

XXXVII.

" I saw—I spied (and laughed in pride),
　　As I skipt o'er yon ruin,"
Said Thatchet-thorn, holding his side,
　　" Twain Gaffers there a wooin'."

XXXVIII.

"Ha! ha! Oh Berry," Thatchet scritched,
  "An elf with hum-drum twisting
The other dainty hoyden witched,
  And she said, 'No resisting!'

XXXIX.

"I feth it was a mouthful speck,
  I wiss to see them"—
             " Hold sir,
Chain thy tongue or I'll instant wreck
  Thy chine, for being bold, sir."

XL.

Thatchet sneak'd off in the crowd
  Under the wing of a fly,
And he tickled the fly's kind shroud,
  For tears came in laughter's eye.

XLI.

" As I gamboll'd and caught the dew,"
  Quo' the Queen,—" to deck our halls,
The prancing gnats my chariot drew
  Above yon ivied walls.

XLII.

"Oh, Lily-tint! Oh, Honey-tongue!
  Such a face and form—so airy,
As were those ruins old among!
  She should have been a fairy.

XLIII.

"And by her side was a hend youth, who
  Was pleading love distressing,
And with harmonious plaining, too,
  He charmed the maid's caressing.

XLIV.

"She is too fair for mortal man,
  Too bright for earthly life,
More formed for elfin joyaunce than
  Queen of a heart-ache strife."

XLV.

("An' ay, besides," cried Thatchet-thorn,
  "'Twill wrath the youth most drearily,
For which I'd spree ten moons to see—
  An' that I would most cheerily!")

XLVI.

" We must save her! we must have her,
  Ere the dews of evening fall,
 On to-morrow, and I'll borrow
  All your freaks to aid my call."
    " Ho! ho!" yell'd, merrily, Thatchet.

XLVII.

" We must save her! we must have her,
  Ere the lovers meet again,
 And we'll bring her, and we'll sing her
  Fairy songs of soothing strain."
    " I fecks we will!" quo' Thatchet.

XLVIII.

" And we'll charm her, but not harm her,
  To forget all ties of earth ;
 For we'll spell-bind, ay, and well bind
  All our arts to cause her mirth."
    " An' I'm your man!" quo' Thatchet.

XLIX.

" We, you Thatchet-thorn commission—
  Thatchet list, you wayward wight—
 To bethink and twist our wish on
  Witching this young maiden bright.
    5*

L.

"Good lack, ah me! ho, ho!—What now?"
  Laughed Thatchet—"*That's* your measure!"
And he smoothed a wrinkle on old Time's brow
  With a loud smack of pleasure.

LI.

The wily, revelling devil, Thorn,
  Swung wild in a cobweb's loop;
A rakish imp as ever was born,
  On the spider he sat with a "Whoop!"

LII.

"All the Spreethogue elves ye ken,
  From Lough Bray to Kill-tipper,
Shall follow Thatchet, through fen and glen,
  To aid the imp to clip her."

LIII.

Thatchet in glee, was tumbling round,
  The cap of a queen-bee's knee;
So joyous was he to be crown'd,
Leading a prank in fairy ground,
  And scritched right gleefully!

LIV.

"Hip, do dun!
 'Tis said—she's won!
I'll smother my feet in the thistle-down,
 Or skate on the snail's bright track,
Or, I'll hide in the pond'rous skin-cloak, brown,
 Flayed from the wood-mouse' back!
Or, I'll straddle on spider's crup, as he weaves
 In the nave of yon ruin his thread—
Or, I'll lie in amidst of two wild mint leaves,
 And roll to a noon-eyed bed.
  I'll watch her—I'll catch her—
   I will! I will!
  Through alley or valley,
   In bower or hill!
I see her! I feel her! I have her! ha, ha!"
 And he sprang at his joyous note,
 And he laughed, till all doubt
 Such a loud elfin's shout
 Leaped from an elfin throat.

LV.

"Ha! ha!"—laughed he, as he woke the light
 Of a star that slept on the pavement,
 And he tumbled him round
 To a jocular sound,
Regardless of court behavement.

LVI.

"Hey, in the ruin,
Lovers will be wooing,
 Little guessing,
 In caressing,
What the elves are doing.

"Hey, in the even,
 Lovers will be grieving,
 Little knowing
 What is growing
For their hearts' deceiving.

"By the set of sun
 To-morrow, she's won!

"For o'er the bog,
 Or through the fog,
 Under the hill,
 Over the rill,
 In the moonlight,
 Or the noonlight,
 Bat's wing riding,
 Owl's beak chiding,
 On Pooka prancing,
 Or star-light dancing,

Whatever ye wot
On earth, or be not,
Eft soon that it *is*,
For Thatchet, I wis,
Is the sprite that is here
To eke whatever ye ken!
For aught be it murky, or yea be it clear—
I'm slave to the Queen o' the glen!
Be it done in a moon's or sun's career,
I'm slave to the Queen o' the glen!"

LVII.

" Hail to our Cleena, Queen o' the glen,"
Shouted the elves and fairy land then,
Up took the echo, and out-sped again—
" Hail to our Cleena, Queen o' the glen."

PART FOURTH.

I.

The night is gone, the morning past,
　　And that noon dead forever;
And evening comes, like a shadow cast,
　　Time's brighter tints to sever.

II.

An evening like the yester one,
　　A calm and balmy eve,
Like nun, afraid that sighing tone
　　Would make her bosom heave.

III.

All was still as a sleeping fair,
　　Placid with heav'nly dreaming,
Whose visions of bliss to her fancy were
　　Double their actual seeming.

IV.

The gentle Eva forth had sped,
　To meet her idoll'd lover;
The daisy bent not beneath her tread,
　As Innocence did above her.

V.

Two genial faces-under-a-hood,
　Drinking the welcome dew,
Seemed, in a joy of brotherhood,
　Toasting her beauty too.

VI.

The Cowslip and the Buttercup,
　They bowed a silent bliss,
And Forget-me-not, in the lonely spot,
　Stole from the sod a kiss.

VII.

Fond memory's emblatic elf,
　He noted the passing one,
And kissed, in lieu the charmer's self,
　The ground she trod upon.

VIII.

And thus the plants, in each other's joy,
  Show how they felt for hers,
And kissed once more, as she tript o'er,
  With the zeal of worshippers!

IX.

The meadow-sweet waved like a bridal plume;
  And the streamlet by the path
    Kept on a wild pace,
    To be sunn'd by her face,
Such radiance its beauty hath.

X.

Now was her heart a brimful cup,
  With Love's delicious presence,
And thoughts of Kevin bubbled up
  To the top of the sparkling essence.

XI.

Her bearing bright, her footstep light
  As a May-wafted feather;
She seemed a humanized delight,
  As skipt she o'er the heather.

XII.

And oh, why should she not present
  Incarnate love and rapture?
Loving and loved—with two joys sprent,
  Yielding, and making a capture!

XIII.

'Tis only thus that true Love's years
  Roll free of pain and sin—
The sin of doubt: who happy wears
  Love's crown, must yield to win.

XIV.

And oh! Heaven help the loving heart
  That meets no love in turn,
And send its light, to save from blight
  That passion-bursting urn.

XV.

The heart that links unto a heart,
  Unknowing if it beats,
May never find, its once clear mind,
  And peace it never meets—
Earth has no future for its kind;
  No past, but killing sweets.

XVI.

But Eva, blessing in her love,
　　Was bless'd in her adorer;
The present seem'd but as Peter's gate
　　To the heavenly fate before her.

XVII.

As moved she down the hilly side,
　　Like blossom weather-wafted,
Crowning the air with double pride
　　Of fragrance then engrafted—

XVIII.

A charming strain falls on her ear,
　　A thrilling measure 'tis,
And tender, too.　She stay'd to hear—
　　"Ah! yes, 'tis surely his!

XIX.

"Ah, yes—it must be Kevin's harp!
　　It is that love-lorn strain
He often plays."　She eager stays
　　To catch the loved refrain.

XX.

And yet she stays: adown her head
    Low bent, as joyed she grew,
And hands upraised, as though they said—
    "Hush, birds, and listen too!"

XXI.

The strain swept on—sweet harmony—
    The maiden soul held still,
As though each magic symphony
    Could chain or free at will.

XXII.

"Now shall I give my love surprise!"
    And round she sprang in glee;
But nothing there stood proof her eyes,
    And wonder-struck was she.

XXIII.

Wonder struck was the maiden young,
    At her deceit of ee;
But a voice yet sung, and a harp still rung,
    And still the strain hears she.

XXIV.

Yea, still its ripples lave her ears,
　More dulcet than before,
And every wave of sound she hears
　Is met by an eager shore.

XXV.

Now plaintive rose the witching lay,
　And now a subdued splendor
Trids the dulcet anguish through,
　So passionately tender:

XXVI.

And now a voice of sadness pours
　Its soul upon the air;
While the maiden stays as one delays
　On last words of a prayer.

(.i.)

Where is my darling—
　Oh, where is her shadow?
　Is she in the meadow,
Singing with the starling?
6*

Is she by the river?—
  Is she mid the trees?—
Ah! my heart is ever
  Searching her and ease.

(II.)

I've heard the starling,
  I've been in the meadow,
  But saw not the shadow
Of Eva my darling.
  She's not by the water—
    She's not in the wood—
  Thro' the trees I've sought her,
    And down by the flood.

(III.)

I told the starling
  To sing out my maiden;
  Robin, too, is laden,
With news for my darling;
  And the little sparrow
    That chirps in the thatch,
  And swallow, fleet as arrow,
    Go my love to catch.

(IV.)

I told the starling,
　　Sparrow, and the swallow,
　　Ere they went to follow,
Where *I'd* meet my darling:
　　Not in fields of clover,
　　　Neither in the bower,
　　Nor by rushing rover,
　　　But *here*, at this hour.

XXVII.

" Now shall I give my love surprise!"
　　And round she tript in glee;
But nothing there stood proof her eyes,
　　And wonder struck was she.

XXVIII.

But still the air with song is fraught,
　　Making sweet the gloaming;
'Tis plain the singer's anxious thought
　　But echoes to his roaming.

XXIX.

"Not in fields of clover,
　　Neither in the bower,
　　Nor by rushing rover,
　　But here, at this hour."

XXX.

Now Eva deftly stole along—
　　Softly crept the maiden—
Aside the brake, the shrubs among,
　　Her breath love-ful laden.

XXXI.

Scarcely breathing crept she, listening—
　　Catching whence the sounds arose;
Her love-laughing eyes were glistening,
　　At the sight they will disclose.

XXXII.

Her thoughts were laughing amongst them-
　　selves—
　　To steal so—such a treat! .
Little thought she, the airy elves
　　Were laughing at Love's defeat.

XXXIII.

Little she dreamt that an elfin harp,
　　Tuned to a mortal ear,
　　　　Was pilf'ring the store,
　　　　At the sill of Love's door,
And making the door a bier.

XXXIV.

"Not in fields of clover,
Neither in the bower,
Nor by rushing rover,
But here, at this hour."

XXXV.

More sorrowful the voice became,
　In grief at her not coming;
Now near it wails, in a tone of blame,
　Now at a distance humming.

XXXVI.

Behind her once it moaned in pain,
　And then it crooned before her;
By her side, anon, as though the strain
　Would weave a madness o'er her.

XXXVII.

On she sprang, with Hope's wild strength—
　Round she trod the strain:
To right trod she—to left trod she,
　And trod all o'er again.

XXXVIII.

Till wearied out, her tender frame,
　　By longing hope deferred,
She sank down on the spot—the same
　　Where first the tune she heard.

XXXIX.

As though her mother Earth would bear
　　Some comfort to her dearth,
As Indian catches in his ear,
The presence of some mortal near,
　　By listening to the earth.

XL.

And thoughts rose up within her lips,
　　To tell what anguish wrung
Her heart, but fell, as fountain drips,
　　Back to whence they sprung.

XLI.

For beat her heart so piteously,
　　No word could dare essay,
To fill its grief, or sorrow dree,
　　Or soothe its woes away.

XLII.

And as she lay, the song once more
   Burst in upon her swoon,
As the mystic fire that revels o'er
   The dismal-faced lagoon :

XLIII.

"Not in fields of clover,
   Neither in the bower,
Nor by rushing rover,
   But here, at this hour."

XLIV.

And as bright morning bursts from night,
   Sweet words escaped her gloom--
" And *I am here*, my Kevin dear,
   I'm thine unto the tomb."

XLV.

Her thought so spread her lifeless form,
   It shook her till she wake ;
And lo! as sun o'er March cloud dun,
   Her love bounds o'er the brake.

XLVI.

And quickly raised was Eva fair,
   Unto his sheltering heart ;
And nestling there, as thought in speech—
The heaven she had pined to reach—
   She prayed they " never part."

XLVII.

" And are you mine?"
           " Thine, only thine!
Ay, darling youth, forever!
The earth holds not, so fair a lot,
   That could me from thee sever!"

XLVIII.

" Oh, speak on yet—my Eva, yet—
   Why should such sun-thoughts dally:"
" I am thine," she cried, " while the sky is blue,
Or the Dodder its Glan-nis-mole sings through;
While the seasons roll, and the loving birds
Warble to each their aërial words!
Though death should come, my love still true,
As the tree to the sod from which it grew—
While those darling hills—those elf-bound hills,
Embrace with calm shadows their offspring rills,

Or Kippure, like an aged parent fills
 The throne of state,
  With pride elate,
And fatherly views the valley!"

XLIX.

" Mine—*only* mine?"
     " Forever thine!"
 And she clung around the youth
With the fervor which betrays itself,
 Supporting a woman's truth.

L.

He kissed her, and excess of joy
 So wrought, when strength had gone,
She felt that dizziness which doubts
 The fact one gazes on.

LI.

She felt as lifted from the sod
 Into his dear embrace—
But were it clouds her Kevin trod,
 She'd tread the self-same place.

7

LII.

Half waking from her swoon of heart,
　　She feels her in the air,
Mid myrial crowds that nimbly part,
　　To make her pathway there.

LIII.

Around, the sky—below, dim void—
　　And up she's onward driven:
'Tis a dream, like those her childhood enjoyed—
　　Dreaming of going to heaven.

LIV.

But round quaint little spectrés flit,
　　Like motes in her bright splendor;
With jocund songs and gleeful wit,
　　And fragile shapes so tender.

LV.

And hither they run, and thither they run,
　　In vain their glee to smother;
And air looked a moving mine of gems,
　　As they pelt dew at each other.

LVI.

She clasped her arms about the youth,
  To feel had she been sleeping,
Full pure in confidence and truth,
  Of safety in his keeping.

LVII.

'Tis surely all some witching dream,
  Else her eyes need heart's upbraiding,
For Kevin, like the mist on stream,
  From her wild clasp is fading:

LVIII.

As shadow deftly fades away,
  When light approaches clearer,
Her opening gaze the maid betrays—
  No youthful Kevin's near her.

LIX.

The shape she prest to her maiden breast
  Has dwindled like a flower,
And left but a wizened, withered stem—
She sees the elves—she has heard of them.
Her whole life crowds in a frantic thought,
And crushes her as the truth is caught:

"Oh, hope belied—oh, Love," she cried,
"I have madly leased my soul from you,
While the Dodder runs and the sky is blue!"
 And swooned in the elfin power.

LX.

And wildly laughed imp Thatchet then—
 He roaring and running by fits,
Till e'en the elf-train, thought again and again
 He'd lose his elfin wits.

LXI.

Still alluring, still she follows
 In the love-struck elfin trance,
Far beyond the cloudy hollows,
 To where vagrant planets dance.

LXII.

Once they rested high in the blue,
 To school their wondering care;
And Time a lengthy cobweb threw,
 To teach her to walk the air.

LXIII.

In vast circles gathering round her,
    As the systems round the sun,
Endless splendors hold, astound her—
    Still beginning, never done.

LXIV.

Moving like vast seas of brilliants,
    Each contributing its light
To the forming of a circle,
    That shuts out forever Night.

LXV.

Still revolving, glittering onward,
    High they chant a fairy glee,
As they pass, the echo, gone-ward,
    Answers to her—" Who are ye?"

(I.)

We are Faeries—gleesome Faeries!
    From the haunted raths below ;
We are Faeries—tricksy Faeries,
    From the glistening peaks of snow,

From the far hills to the valley,
　From the valley to the shore,
And from shore to shore we rally,
　Never less, and evermore!
　　　From the far light
　　　　Of Aurora,
　　　From the star-light
　　　　To the earth—
　　　From the sprye-lands
　　　　Of rich Flora,
　　　To the sky-lands,
　　　　We hold mirth!

(ii.)

We may caper on the sunbeam,
　Or rest behind the moon,
When the pleasaunce of our night-dream
　Ushers in a lazy noon;
We raise a monument of dew,
　Distilled from aërial flowers,
And joys like these are waiting you,
　And every charm that's ours.
　　　From the icebergs
　　　　Of.the Vikings—
　　　From the spice-bergs
　　　　Of the East—

To the Prairies,
    Are the likings,
For the Faeries'
    Glorious feast!

(III.)

We may stretch a bridge from pole to pole,
    Wing earth, and all that's in it,
Over the spheres, or round we can roll,
    Or pass through in a minute.
We are Faeries—happy Faeries!
    Giddy, tinted shades of dew:
Whose ever-bursting joy ne'er varies,
    But to double—so shall you!
        From the prismal
           Sun-light glory,
        To the dismal
           Caves of earth—
        From the Flood-god's
           Saga's hoary,
        To the Wood-gods,
           Give us mirth!
We are Faeries—happy Faeries,
    Kings of earth and sea and blue;
Whose ever-bursting joy ne'er varies,
    But to double—so shall you!

LXVI.

"I fecks you will," quo' Thatchet.   "True!
   And if you hest have a mate
Like me," and he kissed young Daisy-dew,
   Who dealt him a box on the pate.

LXVII.

Eva was listless of all earth,
   Enchanting her promised dower;
And her eyes are tinct with elfin dew,
   To give her sight elfin power.

LXVIII.

And soon with the rites of Elfin Land
   They shrive the maid from clay;
And she, in the joy of the fairy band,
   Is not less gay than they.

LXIX.

She revels along as though she ne'er
   Was born out o' the blue,
And floats athrough the loving air,
   Scarce knowing she passes through.

LXX.

And joyously down the azure space,
  They sweep like a stellar shower,
To meet the Queen at the gathering place,
  By the Brocken on Alyagower.

PART FIFTH.

I.

Young Kevin went to the ruin gray,
    Quilted in ivy green,
Where yestere'en his love did pray,
    And Eva's had plighted been.

II.

The young oak branches sighing, bow'd,
    The weird yew wept aghast,
And the ivy leaves, a clustering crowd,
    Shivered as he passed.

III.

The sad old ruin lonely stood,
    A solemn sight to see,
Like one who suffering for his love,
    Longs from the earth to flee.

IV.

Yet there it stood mid the solitude,
  And the wave-like graves so dim,
A beacon rock midst the ghostly flock,
  Beloved unto him.

V.

For to him it brought thoughts of love,
  Of purpose high and pure :
He thankful felt to heaven above,
  And on the earth secure.

VI.

Beneath its calm and holy shade,
  His kindling heart had burned,
And blazed, and spread, until the maid
  Its every glow returned.

VII.

And who, though frosted o'er by Time,
  Or varied fortune, can
Forget the place, where woman's grace
  First made him feel a man.

VIII.

What heart that does not hold the scene,
  As heaven's foretaste here;
The purest, best, that eyes caressed!
  Beyond all others, dear?

IX.

God pity him whose peevish fate,
  Or thoughtless, callous ways,
Cannot with such remembrance mate
  Sweet comfort, bliss, and praise.

X.

And can we wonder Kevin thrilled
  With feelings strangely new,
Where Eva's yearning bounty filled
  The hopes that burned him through.

XI.

The echoes of her blessed voice
  In spreading sounds still seethed
Around the spot, and the youth's heart caught
  So tightly, he scarce breathed:

XII.

Lest with the breathing he might fail
    To catch each fancied tone,
That bade him a life-pathway hew,
Wide and bright enough for two,
    Nor henceforth be alone.

XIII.

The scene, the sounds, the hopes did span
    The youth; till past control
Their mingling pleasures over-ran,
    The chalice of his soul;

XIV.

And burst forth into frenzied speech
    Which he could not suppress:
But what are words to teach, or reach
    The wants of happiness?

XV.

" Ah, happy me! O chosen one,
    Thy fasting eyes prepare,
To feast their hungry glances on
    Thy life-absorbing fair!

XVI.

"Ah, happy me! O proudest one!
  Restrain thy throbbing side:
It swells amain with radiant pain
  Till comes thy radiant bride."

XVII.

Ah, well-a-day, and wo is me,
  That hath this tale to tell:
Would that the elves had left me free
  To break the fairy spell.

XVIII.

The while young Kevin Dhu devoured
  His brain with hopeful bliss;
The gloaming fled, by night o'erpowered,
And the long grass on the dim graves cowered
  Beneath the dew's cold kiss.

XIX.

A shaking off love's lethargy,
  That captive held each limb,
The doubts and tears, of passion's fears,
  In a torrent burst o'er him.

XX.

He wandered up, he wandered down,
　　He counted every tomb;
They seemèd with a ghoulish pith
　　But mimicking his doom.

XXI.

Which way he turned—each tomb he read,
　　Held nothing to his eye,
Save these huge hopeless words of dread—
　　"Sacred to Memory."

XXII.

With startling apathy he took,
　　His eyes from death and clay.
And up into the heavens did look,
　　For some heart-easing ray.

XXIII.

But as to chill his fibres through,
　　And warn his aching sight,
A black cloud, like a hand, came o'er
　　And hid the eye of night.

XXIV.

The weary, sad, suggestive tombs,
  The black and dreary cloud,
The trees like beck'ning funeral plumes,
  The ivy like a shroud;

XXV.

The Dodder's cloud-affrighted waves,
  A moaning, stealthily past,
The winds that wail down the crooked vale
  And burst into gusts at last:

XXVI.

Conveyed to him a weakening sense
  Of desolation near,
Till he scarce could gasp 'neath the icy grasp
  That crushed his heart with fear.

XXVII.

He thought he heard upon the air,
  Around the ruin dim,
Strange voices mutter as in prayer,
  And say—" God pity him."

XXVIII.

His eyes were fraught with helpless power,
  Into the dark saw he;
And he read as plain as at noonday hour—
  "Sacred to Memory."

XXIX.

The Cross, as one with outstretched arms
  And head to heaven, did seem
To tell him that 'gainst charms and harms
  Of earth it was supreme.

XXX.

Upon the youth's bleak ashen heart
  This holy thought did move
The embers, till there leapt apart
  The flames of Faith and Love.

XXXI.

The dark distempers of his brain
  Before his Faith rushed out—
"Oh, dearest love, she'll come again,
  Why—why should I e'er doubt."

XXXII.

" To-morrow I will clasp my fair
 More bright than mountain fay !"
The sky became more overcast,
He shivering Saint Anne's Well past,
The winds grew wild, more black the sky,
And the shaggy trees, as he went by,
In mournful dirges called him back ;
But he held on his lonely track,
 Sighing, saying, " Fairest fair,
 More bright than mountain fay !"
And he took himself, though loth to part,
From the spot so dear to his hopes and heart,
 And homeward bent his way.

XXXIII.

Days, and weeks, and months, and years,
 Passed over, and the youth
Still paced the place of love and tears,
 Where he had pledged his troth.

XXXIV.

He there might pace till Judgment-day,
 Pace he might for ever,
For her he sought in the ruin gray,
 Again on earth stood never.

XXXV.

Beneath the Cross in that ruin gray,
  The tombs right fronting where
His Eva sat, his manhood's day
  Passed, talking to the air.

XXXVI.

And oft he played his harp and sung
  The rhymes he used to sing,
And oft her name was on his tongue
  In senseless wandering.

XXXVII.

And when at deep sun-set he played
  Some plaintive air she loved,
He thought the rocks and woods betrayed
  A feeling, and were moved.

XXXVIII.

The hills seemed leaving the dreary posts
  They had sentinelled for ages,
And the ravines aroused their minstrel hosts
  To march with their chiefs and sages.

XXXIX.

To him the vales more wide did gape,
  The Dodder dull had grown,
All things seemed longing to escape
  From him, save the Cross alone.

XL.

And Kevin at its base grown old,
  A life of calm wo passed,
To it he clung, his silent, strong,
  And true friend to the last.

XLI.

Of years threescore, and more, had fled
  Since he with joy nigh dumb,
Went forth to meet his Eva sweet
  And still, he thinks, she'll come.

*   *   *

XLII

It is a glorious close of day :
  In light and shade the rills
Gleam fondly in the ruddy ray,
  That nears the western hills.

XLIII.

In smiles of light, the heath, the rocks,
   Slantwise the sun-beam kissed,
And rested on old Kevin's locks
   Of tangled silver mist.

XLIV.

Anticipating twilight's frown,
   It came by Mercy led,
And wove a supra-mortal crown
   Around old Kevin's head.

XLV.

His spectral fingers o'er the strings
   In trembling labor went;
The minstrel and the minstrel's wings
   Of song, are nearly spent.

XLVI.

Beneath the friendly Cross his soul's
   Dear cause he whisp'ring pour'd;
But sighs like his are organ rolls
   To the ear of Mercy's Lord!

XLVII.

As one who yearns to live alway,
  Eastward he turned his eyes,
With hopes to see from the night of clay
  Eternal dawn arise!

XLVIII.

His night fell on him as he gazed,
  Ere the sun had wholly fled,
And the sun-crown shone—Oh, God be praised!
  O'er the lover-minstrel—dead.

XLIX.

On the spot where he love's passion drank,
  On the gray and wiry moss,
And leaning on his harp, he sank
  In the shadow of the Cross.

NOTES.

1. "Delightful Glan-nis-mole."

—Part I., verse xvi., p. 11.

Glan-nis-mole, or the Vale of Thrushes, a peculiarly wild, romantic, and picturesque valley in the Dublin mountains. Kippure, the highest of this range, lifts its brown head over all the neighboring hills, at the remote end of the valley. On it the river Dodder takes its rise from three springs, which join a short way down, and thence united, springs into the vale, and commences its wild and devious course. The writer tracked the river to its source, and explored the surrounding hills and glens twenty years ago. The

"Ivy-quilted scanty ruin"

(stanza xxiv.) then standing, was the remains of a primitive Christian church, on the right bank of the Dodder. On the opposite bank the rugged hills and table-lands of Alyagower, Kiltipper, Ballymanock, and the yet more wild Castlekelly, are variously prominent. The "Witched Cornaun," one of the Dublin range, better known as the old hill of Rollinstown, and at present called Montpelier, lies to the northeast of Kippure. As suggested by the name, Glan-nis-mole was famous for thrushes, and has been distinguished as the scene of some poems attributed to Ossian. The title of one of these is, "The Lay of the Tall Woman from beyond the Sea, or the Hunt of Glan-nis-mole."

9

2. "The sunbeam is shed, through a rose-leaf, red
    On a neighboring ceanavaun."

                —Part I., verse xxxiv., p. 15.

The ceanavaun, a wild plant, the top of which bears a substance somewhat resembling cotton, and as white as snow.

3. "These crosses, like great note-marks, stand

    *   *   *   *   *

    Referring us to God."

This metaphor was suggested by J. [De Jean] Fraser's lines—

    "The stars are asterisks in Heaven,
      Referring us to God."

4. "His love was fierce as St. Kevin's hate."

                —Part I., p. 22.

The legend of the persistent passion of the fair Kathleen for St. Kevin, and his equally persistent abhorrence of her attention, even to hurling the lovely votaress into the waters of Glendalough, will be remembered by readers of Moore's Melody—"By that Lake whose gloomy shore," and Gerald Griffin's ballad, "The Fate of Cathleen."

5. "His tongue seemed in his fingers."

                —Part I., verse lxxiii.

The expression of the hands, in either delight, hate, agony, or scorn, is most powerful. In Raphael's cartoons, especially in Paul Preaching at Athens, The Death of Ananias, The Sorcerer Struck Blind, we can see the wonderful effect of the expression of the fingers. They are all speaking, and in the words of Shakspeare we may exclaim—

    "I *see* a voice!"

The subject is too suggestive to be more than indicated in a note.

6.   " the mystic Well,
              Blessed by the good Saint Anne."

                                    —Part II., verse x., p. 33.

In a previous volume by the writer " Saint Anne's Well" has been described. A brief extract will be sufficiently explanatory of the allusion in the text:

" The waters are clear and as pure as the soul
    Of the Saint that endowed it.   Beneath a green knoll
    It peacefully slumbers in hallowed repose,
    And though always brimming, it never o'erflows ;
    For a side-long trickle leads off the blest flow,
    When its breast is too full, to the Dodder below ;
    And skirts by the little church Kilmosantan,
    Where the green ivy close the old ruin doth span,
    And clings like a lover whose constancy wages
    A war with old Time—growing fonder through ages !
    On these lonely waters the Saint left a spell ;
    Which faith have the people, and thence to the well
    They fly for its draughts ; for the power Saint Anne
    Bestowed on the spring was, that if mortal man
    Was maimed, ill, but faith had, he'd surely get ease,
    If he creep from the well to the church on his knees."

                            —" Faith and Fancy," pp. 69-70.

Its waters are deemed not less efficacious if they can be partaken of by a purgatorial sufferer.

7. " Honey-tongue and Folks-glove."

                                    —Part III., verse xvi., p. 45.

Folks-glove, the fairy, or wee folk's glove. The flower commonly called fox-glove.

8. " And fairy seannachies with beards
　　Of silver thistle-down."
　　　　　　　　　　—Part III., verse xxiii., p. 46.

Seannachie, an ancient historian or story-teller.

9. " And all ye that wraithe Glancree,
　　Or guard the lonely haunted Loughs."
　　　　　　　　　　—Part III., verse xxxiv., p. 50.

Glancree, a wild and eminently romantic locality. The loughs
alluded to are the contiguous lakes, but which are known as
"Lough Bray." There are two, the upper and lower. The latter
is the more picturesque. It is wild and solitary, situated up in
the mountains, and presents evidence warranting the belief that
it is the crater of an extinct volcano. The fairies have great
repute hereabouts